LET'S COUNT GOATS!

words by
Mem Fox

goats by
Jan Thomas

BEACH LANE BOOKS • New York • London • Toronto • Sydney

Here we see a mountain goat frisking in the sun.

And here we see a city goat
going for a run.

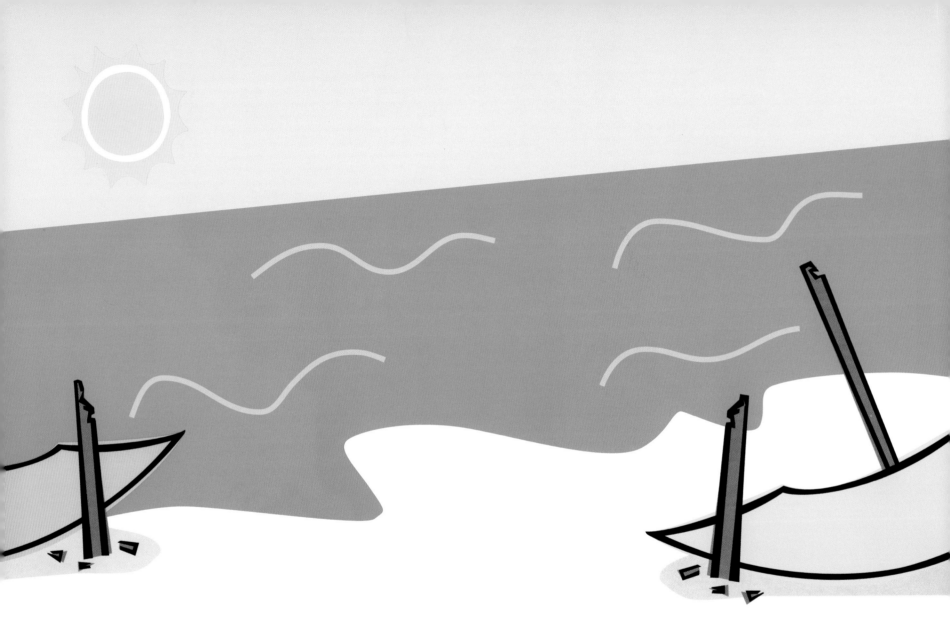

But can we count the **SEASIDE** goats?
(I think there's only one.)

Here we see
a drinking goat.

And here a goat is eating.

But can we count
the **LITTLE** goats,
lost and loudly bleating?

Here we see an airport goat looking for her cases.

But can we count the **PILOT** goats with goggles on their faces?

Here we see a show-off goat playing on the bars.

But can we count the **ROWDY** goats careering round in cars?

Here we see an over goat.

And this one's going under.

Here we see a sandpit goat playing with his toys.

But can we count the **TRUMPET** goats making all the noise?

Here we see a summer goat
with nothing left to mow.

But can we count
the **WINTER** goats
huddled in the snow?

Here we see a fireman goat climbing through the smoke.

But can we count the **RESCUED**

goats trying not to choke?

Here we see a soccer goat roaring at the ref!

But can we count the **CHEERING** goats who must be going deaf?

Here we see the story goats
and all their shining eyes.

Now . . .

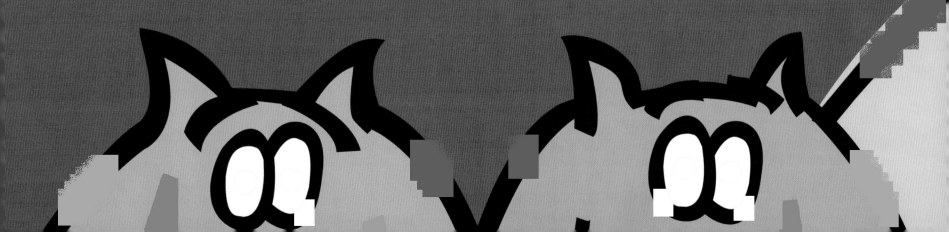

can you count
their pricked-up ears?

You can?